ENCOUNTERS BIGFOOT

VOLUME 1

ETHAN HAYES

FREE REIGN

CONTENTS

INTRODUCTION

Welcome to *Encounters: Bigfoot,* a collection of gripping stories exclusively dedicated to the legendary creature known as Bigfoot or Sasquatch. In this book, I'll present chilling eyewitness accounts, these stories will take you on a thrilling journey into the heart of the Bigfoot phenomenon.

You may wonder why this book focuses solely on Bigfoot and Sasquatch when my previous works explored a variety of cryptids and supernatural beings. The answer lies in the sheer magnitude of fascination and intrigue that surrounds these elusive creatures. Bigfoot, with its towering presence and enigmatic nature, has captivated the imaginations of people across the globe for decades. It has become a cultural icon, woven into the fabric of folklore and urban legends.

Throughout history, tales of encounters with Bigfoot have been shared, passed down through generations, and whispered in hushed tones around campfires. These stories transcend cultural boundaries, appearing in different forms and under various names in different parts of the world. But the essence remains the same—a towering, hairy creature lurking within the depths of forests, leaving behind footprints and a lingering sense of awe.

By dedicating this book solely to Bigfoot and Sasquatch, we can explore the complexities and nuances of these encounters in greater detail. Each story offers a unique perspective, shedding light on the profound impact these encounters have on the witnesses' lives. From heart-pounding sightings in remote wilderness to inexplicable vocalizations echoing through the night, these stories reveal the profound effect that an encounter with Bigfoot can have on the human psyche.

It is my hope that this collection will entertain, enlighten, and fuel the curiosity of those who have been captivated by the mystery of Bigfoot. Whether you approach these stories as a skeptic, a believer, or simply a lover of the unknown, prepare to embark on a journey

that will challenge your perceptions, ignite your imagination, and leave you contemplating the existence of
one of the greatest enigmas of our time—Bigfoot.

So, gather around, dear readers, and prepare to
immerse yourself in the world of *Encounters: Bigfoot*.
Open your mind, keep your senses sharp, and let these
stories transport you into a realm where the line
between fact and folklore blurs, and the truth lies
hidden amidst the shadows of the forest.

Ethan Hayes

CHAPTER ONE
VISIT FROM A FEMALE BIGFOOT

LET ME TAKE YOU BACK TO A MEMORABLE CAMPING TRIP I HAD just a few months ago, in the beautiful wilderness of South Carolina. It was September, a time when the colors of nature begin to change, and the air carries a hint of anticipation for the approaching fall season. Little did I know that amidst the serenity of the remote campground, an encounter awaited me that would defy all expectations and leave an indelible mark on my mind.

As the evening settled upon the campsite, and the sky transformed into a canvas of twinkling stars, a peculiar tapping sound reverberated from above—the roof of my trusty camper. It was as if unseen fingertips were gently rapping against the metal surface, creating an eerie symphony that disrupted the tranquil night.

Curiosity mingled with a tinge of apprehension, urging me to investigate the source of this mysterious disturbance.

Stepping out of the camper, the cool night air enveloped me, carrying with it a sense of anticipation and the faintest whisper of something out of the ordinary. And then, I heard it—a soft, rhythmic sound that seemed to mimic the act of breathing, but with an enigmatic quality that defied explanation. It was an ethereal, elusive melody that tantalized my senses, making it difficult to put into words. I strained my ears to grasp its essence, to decipher the nature of this elusive phenomenon.

In the dimly lit surroundings, barely 15 to 20 feet away, stood a figure that seemed to have emerged from the realm of myth and mystery. It was a creature, unmistakably female, bearing a striking resemblance to both a gorilla and a person. My eyes widened in disbelief as I took in its surreal appearance—the gorilla-like breasts juxtaposed against the partially human face. It was a sight that defied the boundaries of what I believed to be possible, challenging my perception of the natural world.

As if sensing my presence, the creature emitted a soft, soothing cooing noise—a sound that resonated deep within my being. It was a tender, maternal murmur, reminiscent of a mother comforting her young. In that moment, time seemed to stand still as the creature turned gracefully, disappearing into the protective embrace of the nearby treeline. I stood there, awestruck and bewildered, grappling with the sheer strangeness of what had just unfolded before my eyes.

The sheer size of the creature added to the surrealness of the encounter. Standing at a towering height of approximately 8 feet, it possessed a majestic presence that commanded attention and respect. Its massive form, shrouded in the veil of the night, left an indelible imprint on my memory. I had entered the wilderness with a sense of adventure and a longing for the unexpected, but I could have never fathomed coming face to face with such a marvel.

The cooing noise, reverberating in the air, lingered like a haunting melody. It was unlike anything I had ever heard before—an enigmatic chorus that seemed to resonate from the depths of the creature's being. Its unique timbre evoked a sense of both familiarity and unease, leaving me pondering the mysteries of the natural world.

As the creature gracefully retreated into the darkness, a profound sense of wonder engulfed me. I struggled to comprehend the enormity of what I had just witnessed—a glimpse into a realm where the boundaries of reality blur, and the extraordinary coexists with the ordinary. It was a moment that defied explanation, leaving me humbled by the vastness of the universe and the countless wonders it holds.

In the days that followed, I found myself revisiting the memory, contemplating its significance and seeking solace in the company of fellow campers who shared the experience. Each retelling of the encounter only deepened the mystery, as others recounted their own encounters with strange tree formations in the forest— a puzzle that remained unsolved, leaving us all yearning for answers.

As I sit here now, recounting the tale, the memories still vivid in my mind, I am left with a profound sense of gratitude for the remarkable experiences that the natural world has to offer. It is a reminder that, no matter how much we think we know, there will always be mysteries that elude our understanding, inviting us to embrace the unknown and approach life's adventures with an open heart and a curious spirit.

CHAPTER TWO
NONSENSICAL NOISES

IT WAS SEPTEMBER 17TH, 2005, AND I'M SITTING IN MY DEER blind, minding my own business, when out of nowhere, I start hearing this bizarre gibberish hollering. I mean, seriously, it sounded like a bunch of nonsensical noises coming from behind me, roughly a hundred yards away.

Now, you might think, "Ah, it's probably just some wildlife or maybe some rowdy teenagers messing around." But let me tell you, this wasn't your ordinary woodland creature or prankster. This gibberish hollering, it started moving, y'all. It was heading from east to west, getting closer and closer to where I was sitting. And let me tell you, that's when things started to get real unsettling.

Feeling a mix of curiosity and nerves, I unzipped the

back of my deer blind and grabbed my trusty field glasses. I wanted to get a glimpse of whatever was causing such a ruckus and scaring away the deer. But guess what? When I peered through those glasses, there was nothing to be seen. Nada. Zilch. It was as if this bizarre noise had no visible source. Now, that's enough to make anyone's heart skip a beat.

As if the situation wasn't unnerving enough, the sound kept getting closer, and my anxiety levels started to skyrocket. Mind you, I had all the proper permissions to be hunting in that area, but that didn't stop the fear from creeping in. And that's when it hit me—literally hit me—the most peculiar stench I've ever encountered. It was a mix of damp, musty roadkill and, believe it or not, dirty diapers. Yeah, I know, it sounds repulsive, and trust me, it was.

The combination of the advancing noise, the invisible presence, and the ghastly odor forced me to make a quick decision. I had to prioritize my safety above all else. Without wasting a moment, I readied my bow, nocked an arrow, and made a swift exit from the deer blind. Fear wrapped its icy fingers around my heart as I made a beeline away from the disturbance, not daring to look back.

But here's the kicker, folks. As I emerged from the woods, heading toward my trusty vehicle parked approximately twenty-five yards away, I heard it again. That gibberish hollering was still going on, but this time it was coming from the parallel woods, about twenty yards from where I was. Can you imagine? It felt like I was being trailed by an invisible tormentor, and let me tell you, that sent shivers down my spine like nothing before.

At that point, panic took over, and I wasn't taking any chances. With my bow firmly drawn and ready for action, I sprinted towards my truck. I was ready to defend myself against whatever unseen force was doggedly following my every move. Yet, despite my heightened senses and the intensity of the situation, there was still no sign of anything—no movement, no figure lurking amidst the trees. It was as if I was being pursued by a ghost.

Finally, I reached my truck, my heart pounding in my chest. I quickly released my bowstring without letting the arrow loose, placing my bow carefully in the back seat of my trusty Suburban. With adrenaline coursing through my veins, I fired up the engine and wasted no time in making my exit. I can tell you this, folks, in all my years of hunting bears, wild pigs, and deer, never had I experienced such a gut-wrenching need to flee the woods.

So, there you have it, folks, the unforgettable tale of

my eerie encounter in the swamp bottoms of West River. It was a day that forever changed the way I view the wilderness, reminding me that even amidst the beauty and tranquility of nature, unseen forces can stir, evoking fear and uncertainty.

CHAPTER THREE
MIGHIGAN ENCOUNTER

My son-in-law and I were out running our hounds on a coon hunt that night. The area we were in stretched far beyond Green Lake, extending into the Hickey Marsh and eventually reaching the Seney. Little did we know that this particular night would be etched in our memories forever.

As we parked our vehicles, preparing for the hunt, I couldn't help but notice the remains of partridges scattered around. It didn't strike me as anything out of the ordinary at the time. Our hounds, full of energy and excitement, were eager to get started. I released a young and proven hound, both displaying immense determination and fearlessness. Something in my gut told me that we might not be chasing coons that night; it felt more like a bobcat was on the prowl.

Sure enough, after about twenty minutes, the hounds signaled they had treed. We made our way towards them, but just before we reached the tree, the creature bailed, much like a cat would when it catches sight of lights at night, or a bear when we pursue them. Undeterred, the dogs pulled themselves together and resumed the chase, leading us deeper into the wilderness.

Sensing the need for caution, my son-in-law decided to return to the truck, ready to call me out if necessary. I kept the tracker with me, venturing further into the marsh, where a dense blend of spruce, cedar, bog, and popple surrounded me. The dogs had treed deep within this maze of foliage. In search of a vantage point to better hear their barks, I climbed a high spot— a thickly wooded ridge. My radio tracker struggled to pick up their signals, as well as the extra collar left at the truck. Its range in such densely forested areas was limited to around 7 miles. I slowly swung the tracker, hoping to catch a stronger reading.

Amidst the hunt, a foul odor wafted through the air. At first, I dismissed it, assuming it was simply my own scent after multiple encounters with swamp muck. But as I swung the tracker, its coonlight illuminating the path of the antenna, my gaze fell upon a pair of eyes nestled among the spruce trees, right next to a deer trail on the ridge. As a seasoned coon hunter, I had seen my fair share of eye shine in the darkness. However, this sighting gave me pause. I shrugged it off momentarily and swung the tracker back, only to find the trail before me filled with a creature standing merely twenty feet away.

This being stood at an astonishing height of around 8 feet, boasting long arms with distinct fingers, a barrel chest, and a potbelly. Its eyes, deeply set and intense, locked onto mine, while its mouth hung open. Strangely enough, its ears appeared small in proportion to its massive frame. Time seemed to stand still as I stood frozen, my hounds' call forgotten in the face of this surreal encounter. I couldn't tear my eyes away as the creature wrapped its hand around a large spruce tree. Its hair, a blend of black and brown, was neither long nor short, while its nose appeared flat, and its face lacked the same hair coverage as its body. I can't quite recall how it departed from the scene, but the lingering smell followed me almost all the way back to the truck, where my son-in-law met me. He jokingly commented about me passing gas, unaware of the terror that had just unfolded.

Shaken to my core, I struggled to regain composure as we made our way back, doubting the accuracy of my tracking system and questioning the reliability of my compass. The path we took back wasn't the straightest; the encounter had left me disoriented. To this day, I haven't mustered the courage to run my hounds in that area again, whether it be for coons or bears. Moreover, it remains the only time I have left my beloved hounds alone in the woods. The following morning, after getting some much-needed rest, I ventured back up there, my nerves on edge, in a desperate attempt to locate my hounds by myself, as my son-in-law had to go to work. Thank the Lord, I found them treed in the beechwoods, just 30 feet off the gravel road, with the most beautiful sleeping bobcat perched in the tree.

CHAPTER FOUR
SASQUATCH CABIN

I HAD LIVED ON THOSE MOUNTAINS FOR FIVE YEARS BEFORE THE incidents began. There was nothing notable at first, little things here and there. Things moved around the property; animal carcasses left hanging in trees. They started in spring and continued into winter before I left. The big thing that happened that caused me to move out of my home and live back in the city happened one especially cold winter weekend.

I woke up early Friday morning. Staring up at the wooden ceiling for a bit before I sat up. The fire from last night died down but the heat still hugged the air like a blanket. I stood and stretched, walking into the living room, and adding some wood to the fireplace. I stoked the fire, made sure it took again before I made my way over to the kitchen. I decided to splurge a little and made bacon, eggs, toast, and some pancakes. Whilst I was eating, I looked out at the complete whiteout from the large window. The storm had been raging for a couple days at that point, the snow was halfway up my calves. I finished breakfast and washed up the dishes before I got into my snowsuit and pushed open the door. The blast of cold could be felt down to my bones, shivering. I trudged out, fighting against the snow. Each step felt heavier than the last. It took me a while to make it across the clearing to the small shed where I kept the snow blower. I was trying to open the shed when I noticed something strange off to my right. I squinted trying to make it out. After a while, I still could not see it clearly and started to trudge towards it. When I got to the tree line, I was shocked to see a deer hanging in the tree. I was used to this by now, but it was never anything as big as a deer. I felt my mouth run dry, deep tracks in the snow left by a bipedal creature. I twisted the deer, trying to pull it down, I fell back when I noticed a jagged hole in the stomach. I took a few deep breaths before making my way back to my feet. I grabbed the carcass and pulled it down, putting it over my shoulder. I carried it back to the shed, pulling the door the rest of the way open. I dropped the deer onto the butchering table and grabbed my knife. I had spent many days hunting and learnt many skills when it came to skinning and cleaning animals. I took care to check on the skin and insides, once I made sure it was safe, I tied its legs together and hung it up in the corner on a hook.

Grabbing the snowblower, I started it up and pushed my way out of the shed. The storm kept dumping more snow, falling in large clumps. Even as I made a path to my front door, the snow was settling, my thoughts roamed back to the deer carcass. The deep tracks, even in the tree line, looked fresh. I did one more pass with the snow blower before putting it away. Grabbing a bit of firewood, I headed back inside. I shook off the snow and tossed the wood to the side. I got out of my snow gear and made my way to the window. I looked out, but could no longer see the trees, simply a white sheet. I watched for a while, putting on some coffee. The snowfall slowed for a bit while I poured myself a cup, I could start to make out the tree line as I took a tentative sip of the hot drink. I leaned forward as it came into view; it was at this moment that I saw the creature for the first time. I could barely make out anything other than an outline. But what I saw was ingrained into my memory forever. It walked on two legs; it was also tall with thick arms and legs. I couldn't make out what it was wearing. Although it looked like it had fur clothes. I watched as it walked along the tree line towards the shed. It was at this time that I noticed he did not have clothes but thick fur. My breath started to increase, watching closely as the creature walked up to the shed and stopped in front of the door. It raised its arm and swung it at the shed door. The cold wood easily shattered under the force of the punch. I could hear a roar come from the creature as he entered the shed. The creature returned after a minute; the deer carcass was being dragged from behind. As the creature stepped outside, it looked towards the house and I could have sworn we locked eyes, it was for a moment but through the storm, I saw a flash of two dark eyes staring at mine. I took a step back, quickly turning to the bedroom and going for the satellite phone I keep in my nightstand. I took it out and turned it on, walking back to the window. At this point, the storm had picked back up and the creature was gone. I heard the beep of the phone finishing its startup sequence, bringing it up. My heart dropped, there was no signal. The storm clouds were blocking the signal. I tossed the phone on to the couch. A fear of what I had seen creeps inside. I have never frightened easily but the way that creature looked at me, its sheer size, terrified me. I walked up to the front door and checked that it was bolted. I slid a dresser in front of the door. There was no way to get down the mountain in this storm and I couldn't call for help. Barricading myself inside and waiting for the storm to die was the safest option. I checked outside before closing the blinds. I walked over to the couch, kneeling, I reached under and pulled out a case, I opened it to find my hunting rifle. I took it out and loaded up a cartridge. I made my way over to the bedroom, placing a chair in the corner. I sit down and lean the rifle against the wall. Rubbing my hands together, I blew into them. Trying to calm myself down. I don't know how much time passed while I sat there. I could not sit still and kept fidgeting the entire time, waiting for the creature to return. A few times during that wait, I would hear creaks at the front of the house, groans as the wind pushed against the aging wood. Each sound made my heart skip a beat. My thoughts continued to run wild until I eventually passed out in the chair.

I abruptly woke up in the middle of the night, I was shivering and could feel a bitter cold wind blowing through the cabin. I grabbed the rifle and stood up; I aimed it forward as I approached the bedroom door. I slowly peaked out at the dark cabin, as the cold wind cut at my skin like a knife. I didn't hear any other sounds other than the wind as I slowly made my way further in. The fire had died down and so I put down the rifle, I added some wood to bring it back to life. The flames flickered against the bitter cold as the light danced against the walls, leering shadows made it seem as though others were in the room. I approached the table and grabbed my lantern, As I lit it, the shadows faded, and my heartbeat steadied. It was at this point when I noticed a large hole in the main window. A stick had crashed through. My breath catches in my throat, even as the storm raged outside, it was impossible for a stick that size to fly through that window on its own. I approached the window and lifted the lantern, trying to peer into the darkness, but all I saw was falling snow. I felt my hands start to freeze against the bitter wind. So I put the lantern down and Reached for some garbage bags and duct tape. I patched up the window as much as I could, the plastic rippling against the force of the storm.

I put on some soup, rubbing my hands together to warm them up, and waited for it to heat up. I placed my cold hands against the heated metal and greedily drank the soup. My eyes went wild, darting at each little movement in the shadows. I got up and went to grab the chair, bringing it out, I set it next to the fire and sat down. My back was to the wall to keep an eye on the whole cabin. I finished drinking my soup and put it down above the fire. Grabbing the rifle, I cradled it to my chest, finding strength in the cool wood. The fear kept me alert for a few more hours until the bright light of dawn started shining through the cracks not covered by the garbage bag. My head started to droop with the coming day. The tension slowly left my body until I fell asleep.

I woke up with a slight jolt. My rifle fell to the floor, causing me to jump out of my seat. I looked around in a panic, still half out of it. It took a moment for me to get my bearings. I picked up my rifle and set it on the table, I took a few deep breaths before looking out the window. I couldn't help but smile when I saw the blue sky. I quickly ran to the couch and grabbed the satellite phone. I fumbled it as I turned it on, it fell to the floor with a loud crunch and as I lifted it, I noticed a large crack on the screen. I watched in suspense as the screen turned on, I took a deep breath, lifting it up as I waited for a signal. As soon as the phone connected, I quickly dialed up the park rangers who had a station at the bottom of the mountain. When I got through, I explained what happened. Luckily a friend of mine, who I would sometimes hang out with at the cabin when going around, answered. He listened to everything quietly, I finished explaining everything and waited for the response. There was some static before his scratchy voice could be heard. He apologized and explained that they were totally snowed in, and it would have taken a few days to clear a path up. Unless I could come down, I would be stranded. He tried to make me feel better, saying it was probably just a bear, it was easy to mistake these things when you didn't see what I saw. I told him it was not a bear and he said fine, but that didn't change anything. I was still stranded. He told me he would try to get people up as quickly as possible and to stay inside until they could.

After we hung up, I did a quick once over of the cabin to make sure I had everything I needed. There was plenty of food left since I had just recently restocked. The taps were working fine, and I had a couple of jugs as backup. The one thing I did not have a lot of in the cabin was firewood. That was kept in an overhand about 50 feet from the front door. I walked over to the broken window from last night and peered outside through the small parts not covered by the garbage bags. After a few minutes of looking around and not seeing the creature, I decided to run out and grab some wood. I put on all my outdoor gear and made my way to the door. I looked back at my rifle and chose to leave it. I would need both hands to bring the wood back quickly, if anything happened, I would simply run. I took a few deep breaths before I opened the door and stepped outside. The cold hit me like a punch and a shiver shot through my entire body. I began trudging through the snow, keeping my eyes peeled for any movement. My racing heart started to calm down slightly as I reached the overhang without incident. I started placing a bunch of the cut-up wood onto a sled that I kept there, making sure it was full before I began tugging it over the deep snow. I was halfway back when a loud crack like a gunshot rang out beside me. I turned and watched as a large tree fell over some twenty feet beyond the clearing.

It was not uncommon for trees to snap like that in the colder temperatures, but as though it was a warning, whilst I was looking in the direction that the sound came, I once again saw the creature, the trees shaking as it pushed through the underbrush. I began to hyperventilate, tugging hard at the sled trying to move faster. I was almost at the door when I heard the snap of a cord and fell into the snow. I scrambled up and saw that the creature was now in the clearing with me, I completely forgot about the wood and ran back inside, slamming the door shut. I pushed a dresser in front of the door and sat down in my chair holding up my rifle. I waited quietly for some sounds that the creature was trying to get in, but as seconds turned into minutes, turned into an hour, nothing ever came. I put down my rifle and put in the last few pieces of wood I had inside. I slowly opened the door and checked back where I saw it before, but it was gone. I took a few tentative steps out, continuing to closely scan the tree line. I thought I saw movement at one point and dove back towards the door, but it turned out to be nothing. I quickly ran over to the wood and noticed deep fissures in the snow that were not there before. I looked in the direction they went, I could not see anything and began pulling the sled with all my strength until it slid the last few feet to the door. I looked around one more time before starting to pile the wood inside. Once it was all in, I quickly shut the door and barricaded myself inside. I added a couple pieces to the fire and made myself some food. I wasn't very hungry but in that kind of situation, eating to have energy can save your life.

I ate next to the fire, my eyes darting between the door and the window. I looked down, my hands were shaking. Not from the cold, but from the fear and being tense for so many hours. I curled my hands into fists and got up from my seat. I grabbed my rifle and walked over to my room, I grabbed the blankets off the bed and brought them to the couch. I put the rifle down next to the couch and wrapped myself up. I sat there watching as the sun slowly began to set, the day feeling like a blur.

I don't know when I passed out, but the next thing I remembered was being shaken, I slowly opened my eyes and in the blurriness all I could see was brown fur. My mind was engulfed in fear, I tried to reach for my rifle, screaming. But a hand grabbed my wrist, I tried to fight it off, but it didn't let go no matter how hard I tugged. It was at this point that I heard someone calling my name and stopped fighting. I looked up and was surprised to see the ranger telling me to calm down and that it was ok. I stared at him dumbfounded and asked what he was doing there. He let go of me and explained how another storm was fast approaching and so he and a few others grabbed the skidoos and made their way here. When there was no answer at the door, he came in and found me there. I explained to him what happened and as I finished, he nodded, explaining how throughout the years, others have also claimed to see this same creature. I quickly got on all my gear and asked him what they thought it was. He said that no matter how many different people told stories, it always had one name, sasquatch. I looked down at the ground as we made our way out of the cabin, locking it behind us. We went to the skidoos and there were three others waiting for us. I recognized them and we all exchanged pleasantries before making our way down the mountain.

I stayed at the ranger station for the rest of winter. A few of the rangers went up to investigate but were unsuccessful in finding anything. As the snow began to melt, I struck a deal with the men at the station and sold them the cabin to do with as they saw fit. I purchased a small house by the city and never again went back to that cabin. Visiting the rangers was as close as I got.

CHAPTER FIVE
ENCOUNTER IN ALBERTA

I<small>T WAS AROUND TEN YEARS AGO WHEN</small> I <small>HAD AN ENCOUNTER</small> that has stayed with me ever since. Our family has always been fond of camping in the majestic mountains of Alberta, and on this particular trip, we decided to take our trusty old motor home and set up camp in a remote area near David Thompson. It was the kind of place so secluded that we were the only ones there at the time, surrounded by the beauty and tranquility of nature.

Just beyond our campsite, there were numerous bike trails, rolling hills, and vast stretches of forest. Those hills, I would describe them as mini mountains, were quite challenging to climb and surprisingly large in size. My brother, being at that age when relaxation took precedence over exploration, preferred to stay back at the campsite. This left me with the freedom to venture out on my own, biking and hiking to my heart's content.

On one occasion, I decided to grab my Walkman and hop on my bike to explore what I dubbed the "mini mountains." It took me about 20 minutes to reach a point quite far from our campsite. As I pedaled along, lost in the music blaring through my headphones, little did I know that an unsettling moment was about to unfold—one that still haunts me in my nightmares.

I was jamming to some music when suddenly, an eerie sensation washed over me—a distinct feeling of being watched. Startled, I brought my bike to a halt and glanced to my right. At first, all I saw was a large tree stump. But then, out of nowhere, a head peeked out from behind that stump. Time seemed to come to a standstill as I found myself locked in a stare-down with this mysterious figure. It kept shifting its gaze from side to side, as if contemplating its next move. I was frozen, unable to tear my eyes away from the sight.

And then, it happened—the figure stood up. The stump that had initially caught my attention turned out to be as tall as me when this enigmatic being rose to its feet. The sight of it sent shockwaves through my entire being. Something deep inside me screamed to run, to escape from whatever this thing was. In my terrified state, I even lost my balance and tumbled off my bike, leaving a scar on my knee that serves as a constant reminder of that harrowing moment.

The fear coursing through me was palpable, and my pounding heart seemed to drown out all other sounds. When I finally managed to make my way back to our campsite, tears streaming down my face, I couldn't help but pour out my emotions to my parents throughout the entire night. My dad, in his attempt to understand what I had experienced, asked me to take him back to the spot where it had occurred. But the mere thought of returning to that place filled me with such overwhelming dread that I simply couldn't bring myself to do it.

Even to this day, I refuse to camp in that general area. The memory of that encounter, etched deep within my psyche, has left an indelible mark on me, forever altering my perception of the wilderness. It serves as a constant reminder of the unknown mysteries that lie hidden in the woods and the unexplained entities that may inhabit the very places we find solace in.

CHAPTER SIX
INVISIBLE BIGFOOT

When I grew up, I lived in a cabin in the middle of the woods in Alaska. Back in the nineteen seventies when I was a kid, it really was like living feral. We had an outhouse and I remember at a very young age having electricity put into the place for the first time. My parents were simple people, and I was one of seven kids. I was child number five and the loner of the bunch. While my siblings were content to go on all sorts of adventures, in the woods and otherwise, with my parents or each other, I felt much more comfortable in the woods alone. I have since made my living as a writer and author and I guess the making up of strange and oftentimes dystopian worlds and societies started in those woods that surrounded my house when I was little. My parents still live in that house, and I don't live too far from them but nowadays a lot of the land they owned they've since sold off and the place just isn't the same. Not to mention how modernized the house is now. When I was growing up, I had many strange experiences with many things that I still to this day can't explain but one of the strangest and the first was the one I am about to tell you all about now. I always knew that bigfoot existed because even back then there were rumors of the beast among the adults around me. I heard them talking and thought for sure if I hung out in the woods for long enough, I could prove its existence one way or another. My quest started at thirteen and it would take two long years of hanging out in those woods, which I would have been doing otherwise anyway, for me to find what I was looking for. Needless to say, though I greatly underestimated what I was dealing with and never captured proof for anyone but myself.

The day it happened is one I will never forget. I've since seen bigfoot in those woods about a handful of times, but that first time was by far the strangest and it's a memory that sticks out not only because of how odd it all was but also because I know what catching sight of one means, especially nowadays. I packed myself lunch and grabbed some buckets. I was going to try and catch some worms for fishing while I was out there. I had a tree out there that I built a little tree house, which wasn't much of a house really, using sticks and larger pieces of wood that I found. The tree house was quite high, and it overlooked the shore that if you walked through the woods, you would eventually get to. I never expected I would see bigfoot anywhere other than directly inside of the woods too, but that was another shocker. I was digging for worms, and I was close enough to the little beach that I could hear the waves crashing onto the shore, but it was still a long way away from where I was at that point. Everything was normal until I felt like there was someone standing behind me and I started to smell a horrible stench. I looked around but didn't see anyone or anything. I really felt like something was behind me and watching me but for the life of me I saw nothing at all. While looking around to see the reason why I was no longer alone in the forest, I noticed something else odd as well. I noticed that the entire forest seemed to have gone silent. I don't remember noticing exactly when it actually happened, but I noticed it when I felt another presence there with me. It was really creepy and the hair on the back of my neck and on my arms was standing straight up on end. I considered running back home, but I hadn't caught that many worms yet and something inside of me told me that then was my chance to see something out of the ordinary. Remember for two years up until that point I had been trying to obtain evidence that bigfoot existed. I stood up and walked over to a nearby giant tree that had been downed and sat on the stump. I just waited, watched, and listened. There was still total silence and I still felt like I wasn't alone out there anymore.

I tried to pretend like I didn't notice something was wrong or amiss and just started looking at the ground like I was about to go back to digging for worms at any moment. I saw the grass moving to the right of me even though there wasn't any breeze that day at all and from where I was sitting, I couldn't see anything there that would be parting it the way it was. It looked like something large was walking through it all but again, there was nothing there at all. I was scared and my heart started pounding because it was at that point, I knew for a fact that I wasn't alone out there. However, my mind couldn't make sense of what my eyes were seeing or of what it clearly knew at that point; that something invisible was there. Suddenly the birds were chirping again, nothing seemed to be moving around anymore and the feeling of being watched or of not being alone went away altogether. Once again, I thought that I should just go home but I was a precocious and curious teenager, and I wasn't about to just let it go. I needed to figure out what I was dealing with. I heard a really loud whooping noise. It sounded like something hollering and it almost sounded human. Once I heard the first sounds, which were coming from the direction of the shore, I heard the same noises echoing across the forest and through the trees, coming from all over the place. Whatever it was, there were several of them and they were communicating with one another. I ran over to my tree house and climbed up. I was as high as I could possibly go and looked all around. I didn't see anything until I looked over at the beach.

I couldn't believe my eyes as I watched a gigantic beast stand there as it looked around at first. It almost looked like it was making sure it wasn't being seen. It kept turning quickly from one side to the other before it would bend down and pull something out of the water and bring it to its mouth. It was either grabbing small fish, crabs, or clams. I couldn't be sure, but I watched in shock and sheer amazement at the sight. It had to have been about twelve feet tall and maybe five or six feet wide. I could see it very clearly from my vantage point, but it hadn't yet spotted me. I didn't think it would have been able to see me from where it was as I was really far away and so I boldly just stood there, without trying at all to conceal myself, watching this fantastic creature grab its food from the water. It was covered in brownish red fur, all over its body except for its face. Its face was tan colored but had no fur or hair on it. I could see it had large eyes and I think that they were black, but I really couldn't be sure because I wasn't close enough and I still have no real idea. I watched for about ten minutes before it stopped what it was doing again and looked directly at me. I really thought there was no way that it could see me, so I didn't duck or try to hide or anything I just stood there staring at it. It could see me though because it hollered over in my direction and, as though it were talking to or otherwise trying to communicate with something I couldn't see, it pointed up at me. I wanted to duck or get down from the tree stand and run as fast as I could back home, but my legs didn't seem to want to work. I was terrified and my heart sank as I realized it could see me. I bent over for a moment to try and stop myself from passing out and when I looked back up the creature was gone. Well, I could no longer see it anyway. I wanted to go to the beach and look and see if there were any fresh footprints before the tide came in and washed them all away. I didn't have a camera or anything with me but at that point I just needed to prove to myself that I wasn't crazy or seeing things. I needed to prove it to myself that bigfoot existed. There was no question in my mind at that point either of what I had just seen.

I climbed quickly down from the tree and started the somewhat treacherous hike to the beach. I noticed the path I was taking was the same one where I had seen the grass and trees parting and moving earlier, as though someone were walking through it when there was no one and nothing else there. It took me about twenty minutes but finally I made it to the beach. The second I exited the tree line and stepped a foot onto the shore, I felt that strange feeling again like I was being watched. There was no one and nothing there though. That horrible stench was back as I looked around and saw dozens of gigantic footprints all over the sand. There weren't any where I had seen the bigfoot though because the water had already washed them away. It had been standing with its feet in the water as it caught its meal. I was afraid to walk forward because I felt once again like I was being watched and like I wasn't alone. However, there were no other human beings and no animals as far as the eye could see. I heard a loud grunting noise coming from right about where I had seen the bigfoot before and that's when I knew that it was still there, that it had been there all along and that if I went any closer, I would then be approaching it. I also didn't think it was alone and knew somehow deep down inside that it had been a bigfoot that had invisibly walked past me while I was sitting on the stump, and it was more than likely just watching me as I dug for worms as I first recognized that I wasn't alone anymore in the forest.

I turned and ran as fast as I could back to my house. I left the bucket and all the worms I had collected, along with my lunch, in those woods. I never got them back. I was excited but I knew my mom and siblings might not believe me but was hopeful that my father would. However, by the time he got home from work that night it was too late to go trekking through the dark forest and so we waited until morning to walk together to the beach. When we got there nothing was left of the footprints, I had seen there the day before but both of us felt extremely uncomfortable in that area and like we were being watched. Also, I will never forget how strong that horrible smell was when we were out there that day and so many other times too when we were in the woods together or when I was all alone. That's how I always knew a bigfoot was around, even when I couldn't see one with my eyes. My dad believed me, and he would tell the story about when I saw bigfoot on his land, on the shore in the forest, to anyone who would listen. No one dared question or mock him because it would have been considered disrespectful, but I don't think many people believed him. He believed me though and before long he was joining me on my excursions into the woods as much as possible and it didn't take long for us to see one of them while we were together. It was absolutely fascinating and while I know they exist all over the world nowadays, I think Alaska is the perfect place to find one because it really is the last frontier and there is so much untouched land here, even today. I think I figured out and bore witness to a lot of the reason why no one can ever seem to catch a good picture or video and why they aren't able to catch any sort of evidence of its existence and that's that it can disappear or phase out at will. I also believe they make their own portals wherever they stand if they need to and that that's how they get out of there when they feel like a human is threatening them or even just trying to capture photographic or video evidence. Honestly, I think someone trying to catch any evidence of them is threatening in and of itself to a bigfoot but that's just my opinion. I will write about more of my encounters and experiences as well. Just thought that my first experience would be a great place to start.

CHAPTER SEVEN
INDIANA ENCOUNTER

BACK IN AUGUST OF 1985, DURING THE TRANQUIL EVENING hours around twilight, an extraordinary event unfolded while my brothers and I were strolling along the railroad tracks behind our house, heading towards Fort Wayne. Now, Fort Wayne may seem like an unlikely place for a bigfoot sighting, but regardless, I'm here to recount what we witnessed that day.

As we leisurely walked, engaged in animated conversation, and indulged in the classic boyish pastime of throwing rocks, little did we know that our usual track exploration was about to take an unexpected turn. I was just twelve years old at the time, and my oldest brother's keen eyesight caught something peculiar, something that stood out amidst our familiar surroundings. We were well acquainted with these tracks and could instantly tell when something didn't belong. Curiosity piqued, we continued walking towards the enigmatic sight, still oblivious to the significance of what lay before us.

In the waning light of the evening, it appeared to be nothing more than a large mound of black dirt nestled on the left side of the tracks, not far from the rails. Without giving it much thought, we approached it while engrossed in our chatter, absentmindedly kicking stones along the way. Drawing closer, perhaps within a range of 100 to 150 feet, an astonishing sight unfolded before our eyes, shattering our sense of normalcy. To our utter surprise, the mound abruptly stood up, towering on two legs—a colossal figure, easily reaching a height of 7 to 8 feet. With an incredible display of power, it effortlessly cleared a double set of railroad tracks in just two massive strides, swiftly vanishing into the depths of the wooded ravine on the right side of the tracks.

The magnitude of what we had witnessed struck us like a bolt of lightning. It was as if time had slowed down, imprinting every detail of that awe-inspiring moment into our memories. The creature we saw was undeniably tall, standing at a towering height of 7 to 8 feet, its imposing figure defying any logical explanation.

Its upper body was massive and robust, leaving an indelible impression on our young minds.

In a surge of adrenaline-fueled terror, we instinctively turned on our heels and sprinted home as fast as our legs could carry us. Bursting through the door, we breathlessly recounted the encounter to our father, seeking solace and reassurance. As fathers often do, he offered a plausible explanation, assuring us that it was probably just a deer. In the moment, I accepted his explanation, despite the fact that I had never witnessed a deer standing upright on two legs, effortlessly traversing a double set of railroad tracks. However, even to this day, I cannot conclusively claim that it was indeed bigfoot that we encountered. The fleeting glimpse we caught of the creature didn't provide us with a clear view, nor did it emit any of the spine-chilling howls or distinctive sounds commonly associated with such encounters. Nevertheless, one thing remained undeniable—it was an entity unlike any animal we had ever seen before. Perhaps it was merely a man, but if so, he should have secured a place in the record books for his extraordinary abilities.

Allow me to paint a picture of the surroundings to give you a better sense of the setting. The area encompassed the railroad tracks, which were accompanied by gentle slopes and adorned with patches of grass and clusters of small bushes on the left side. On the right side, a stretch of woodland flourished, complete with a slight ravine adding depth to the landscape. There, nestled amidst the woods, you could find a small creek meandering its way alongside a serene pond, enhancing the natural allure of the area.

Once our father was notified of our astonishing encounter, he, like any concerned parent, listened attentively to our tale, offering both his support and a sense of rationality. But deep down, we knew that what we had witnessed that fateful evening went far beyond the realm of ordinary. It left an indelible mark on our young lives, forever fueling our curiosity and leaving us with a sense of wonder about the mysteries that lie just beyond the veil of the known.

CHAPTER EIGHT
COP HAS AN ENCOUNTER

As a law enforcement officer, my commitment to truth and integrity is unwavering. I have no reason to fabricate or exaggerate what I witnessed, and quite frankly, I couldn't care less if anyone believes me. Throughout my career, I've come across stories and rumors of strange phenomena, but I never paid them much attention. It's not that I didn't believe, but rather, I adopted a "seeing is believing" approach.

It happened on a sweltering evening, just after or before Labor Day in 2007. The darkness had descended, roughly around 8:30 or 9:00 PM, although the western sky still retained a faint glimmer, characteristic of that time of year. I was on patrol, driving westbound on Highway 128, leaving Cloverdale behind, responding to a routine alarm call at a ranch property. Such calls were commonplace in my line of work.

As a law enforcement officer, you develop an acute awareness of your surroundings. You notice things that are out of place—a car parked where it wasn't the day before, a person walking along a desolate road, lights emanating from a closed business. These details catch your eye, often escaping the notice of ordinary passersby. And so, as I was driving westbound, something caught my attention—a figure emerging from the ravine and stepping onto the roadside. I can't quite describe it, but I caught a glimpse of movement amidst the brush and instantly knew it was a person. People frequently try to evade us, so my initial thought was that I had startled someone who might be cultivating marijuana in the woods—a common occurrence in these parts. I could discern the outline of a body, and as my headlights reflected off its eyes, it swiftly retreated into the undergrowth before I could pass by.

Believing it to be someone attempting to avoid detection, I slammed on the brakes and promptly reversed my vehicle. That's when I witnessed it in the beams of my headlights. Standing at a height of approximately 6 to 7 feet, it possessed a thick, matted coat of brown fur and walked upright. Although I didn't catch a glimpse of its face as it was facing away from me, the sight left me dumbfounded, just like everyone else who has had a similar encounter. I couldn't believe my eyes. It was certainly not something I was willing to relay over the radio. There were dense branches and over-grown foliage obstructing my view, but there was no mistaking what I had witnessed.

Two details remain etched vividly in my memory. Firstly, the creature had small leaves and grass entwined within its fur all over its back. I observed this as it slowly walked away from me. The image remains seared in my mind. Secondly, I distinctly remember its deliberate and unhurried movements. It proceeded with calculated steps, using its arm to brush aside small branches and twigs obstructing its path. I had the crea-ture in my line of sight from the rear for a significant 4 to 5 seconds before it vanished once again into the thick vegetation. I found myself stepping out of my car, standing there in silence for approximately 2 to 3 minutes, with the engine turned off. I could hear the same measured movements, the unmistakable crunch of leaves and twigs, echoing from the depths below. It seemed to be making its way toward the nearby creek area. Each time the sounds ceased and I contemplated returning to my vehicle, a distant "crunch" would reach my ears, compelling me to linger a little longer, listening intently.

The ravine harbored a creek, and it was evident that the creature had retreated back to that secluded enclave.

Needless to say, I kept my encounter to myself. It was not a matter to be discussed during briefings or recorded in the patrol blotter. Sharing such an experience would undoubtedly have made for an uncomfortable and challenging career. I toyed with the idea of reaching out to one of our Fish and Game Officers, but considering that he was acquainted with many of my colleagues, I decided to maintain my silence. Reading the accounts of others on various forums reassures me that I'm not alone. While I've never encountered a ghost, UFO, or anything of that nature, this experience has opened my eyes to the possibilities that lie beyond the realms of our everyday understanding. It begs the question of what else is out there, lurking just beyond the boundaries of our laughter and skepticism.

CHAPTER NINE
SASQUATCH CANADA

It was that time of the year again, my visit to my summer home in Nakina. Being where I grew up, I made a point to visit at least once a year to go camping, fishing and enjoy the lush forests and lakes. It started off as every other trip did but finished unexpectedly.

I drove into town, music blaring loudly as my girlfriend, and I sang along to the lyrics we knew by heart. We turned down the side road leading to the subdivision where our house resided. Seeing the playground there brought back many fond memories from when I was younger. We pulled into the driveway, and I started to unpack everything while my girlfriend went into the house to air out the place. I brought in our suitcases and set them at the top of the stairs, making my way behind my girlfriend looking out the large front window. I wrapped my arms around her and kissed her head. I could feel her smile as she grabbed my arm. We spoke for a bit to make plans on what we were going to do before splitting off. I chose to run to the northern store in town to pick up some things while she would stay at the house and tidy up. I took a minute to drive there as the wave after wave of nostalgia ran over me. An old restaurant I would hang out at, the train station cafe and many others.

I walked into the Northern, where I was greeted by an old friend of my grandfather. My grandfather spent most of his life there and that was the main reason I was there as well. The friend recognized me from a few years back and asked how I was doing and wanted to know what I had been up to. I explained how I was going camping up on stinger lake. It was my favorite place to fish growing up. He told me a story about when he was younger and driving down the road that led to stinger. He was going fast, but he was sure he saw sasquatch. I thought it was crazy but said how cool that was and that I would keep my eyes open. We said farewell and I went back to shopping. It didn't take me long to get everything before I went back home.

After I got back, I brought everything into the house, kissed my girlfriend and headed back out to get the boat into the back of the truck. Luckily the small twelve-footer we used was light and I had no problem lifting it in and strapping it down. I put in the gas tank and motor before going in and grabbing all our stuff to bring it out. Once everything was loaded, we locked the house again and shot off towards our launch site. It was a bit of a drive, but with the windows down and more music, it felt quick, we arrived and backed down the slope, getting out, I unstrapped the boat and slid it off the truck and into the river. My girlfriend parked the truck off to the side as I got everything ready. My girlfriend came down, hopped into the boat and I pushed us off, jumping in.

The short trip through the river was one of stingers best qualities, all the lush greenery untouched by anyone. We reached the mouth of the river, marked by two trees crossed over. As soon as we cleared it, I lowered the engine fully into the water and we took off. It was around a thirty-minute boat ride to our usual campsite, we saw a couple of moose, a cow and a calf, along the way. But otherwise, we simply enjoyed the sun and wind.

I cut the engine as we reached our destination, jumping to the front of the boat and out, I pulled it up onto shore, tying it to a tree so that it wouldn't go off leaving us stranded. We quickly got everything out of the boat and started setting up camp, I left my girlfriend with the tent and took out the tarp. There were boards nailed to the tree to set up a roof over where we kept the food and mini gas stove. Once that was hanging, I helped finish up the tent and we started a small fire. We grabbed some hotdogs and decided to roast some for lunch. While we were sitting beside the fire, we heard rustling in the bushes behind us. We both turned around quickly and peered into the brush, but whatever made the sound must have gone away quickly since we weren't able to see anything aside from trees and darkness. We didn't think much of it and turned back towards the fire, finishing up our lunch and putting everything away. It was around two pm at this point and my girlfriend wanted to go fishing. Now that the camp was fully set up, I had no problem with that, and we hopped back into the boat. Stinger is a relatively shallow lake and the best way to fish there was to troll, so when we got out further on the lake, I put the motor on low and we began casting out lines. Lady luck was always on my girlfriend's side when we fished together, and that time was no different. To every one fish I caught, my girlfriend would catch three. We kept a few to have supper tonight, but most were tossed back, taking lots of photos, my girlfriend kissing the first as was the ritual.

As the sun began to lower on the horizon, my girlfriend started to get tired and so we decided to call it quits. When we made it back to shore, I tied up the boat, lifted my girlfriend and brought her to the tent, I kissed her and told her she could nap while I cleaned the fish and prepared dinner. She smiled; told me she loved me before settling in. I closed the tent and went back to the boat to collect the fish. I grabbed the filet knife out of my bag and made quick work of the fish. I put the perfect filets onto a plate and made sure to toss the entrails into the lake. It was the best way to keep wild animals like bears away. I cleaned the blood from the board and grabbed my fish batter, I filled a pot with some cooking oil and began properly coating the filets as I waited for the oil to start boiling. Once it did, I tossed in the filets and put some rice on to cook as well. It didn't take long for both to finish, adding a few more logs on the fire and making up the plates of food.

It was seven by this point and I went to wake my girlfriend, slowly stirring her awake with a kiss on the head, I gave our usual, good morning sleepy head, greeting before stepping back out, as I was stretching from being crouched down, I couldn't help but notice a fallen tree off to the side of camp heading inland. I didn't notice it before and upon closer inspection, it looked as though something pushed it over. I tried looking deeper in, but with the sun mostly gone, it was impossible to see anything. I heard movement at the tent and turned around, I made my way over and passed my girlfriend a plate. Enjoying the flaky taste of fresh fish, it had been too long since I had enjoyed this and savored every bite.

Once we finished eating, we tossed our paper plates into the fire and shuffled closer together. I wrapped my arm around my girlfriend's shoulder. We sat like that and listened to the soft sounds of nature as the sun finally vanished for the day, leaving nothing but the small circle of light from the fire and pitch darkness beyond. I kissed her head and suggested we settle in for the night, pouring some water onto the fire, I made sure everything was properly packed up and crawled in after her. We had set a sleeping bag on the ground as cushioning, another on top as a blanket, getting into my pajamas, I crawled in next to my girlfriend and wrapped my arms around her. I wished her a good night and we both slowly drifted off, cuddled in each other's arms. A loud rustling woke me up, I could feel my girlfriend still breathing steadily in her sleep and so checked my watch, it was two in the morning. I looked around the tent, and that is when I heard it again, loud rustling just outside the tent. A bear, I thought to myself and tried to take some deep breaths to calm my heart, but I failed to do so as the rustling got louder. I refused to move. Each passing moment felt like a lifetime. I heard my girl-friend grumble and thought she had awoken, but when I checked, she was still asleep. At this point, the rustling was right outside the tent. Whatever it was, I could hear its breathing, each breath labored and heavy. I held my breath as I heard some brush up against the tent, waiting for it to break in as it stopped. But after what felt like forever, it finally stepped away and I could hear it rummaging through the camp. I watched as some-thing solid hit the tent, making me jump.

The jump caused my girlfriend to stir awake and I quickly put my hand over her mouth to stop her from saying anything. I whispered softly that something was outside and she must have heard it as well, since she stopped moving. It continued making a ruckus for a bit longer before it finally left. I sighed in relief and finally let go of my girlfriend. She turned to me and asked me what that was. I told her I didn't know but most likely a bear. Since they weren't uncommon in these parts of the woods. We laid there in silence and listened in case it came back, but as the sun began to rise, there were no more incidents.

I slowly opened the zipper to the front door once it was bright enough for us to see without issue, popping my head out of the hole. I looked around the camp but didn't see anything amiss aside from our food being tossed all over. I opened the door the rest of the way and crawled out of the tent. Stretching as I took a better look around. The cooler holding all of our food was opened, the lid tossed far to the side. Most of the food was out and tossed all over the place, a lot of the meat we brought like sausages and bacon were gone. The heavy thing that hit the tent before was a pack of hotdogs, left relatively untouched, I checked that the water was fine and gave the okay for my girlfriend to come out. She crawled out shortly after and saw the mess. She helped me collect everything and clean up. We checked everything and luckily a lot that had been tossed aside was still good to use and eat. I put a kettle on to boil and sat down with my girlfriend to discuss what we wanted to do. Bears were in the area, but if we were careful, they weren't a threat. So, we could stay, But if she didn't want to, I was ok with heading back. I heard the kettle go off and got up, making some tea. I passed a mug of it to my girlfriend and waited for her choice.

After some thought we decided to give it one more day and then we would cut the trip a day short. We had traveled so far to do this; it would be a waste to cut the trip so short. I kissed her head and nodded before getting up to grab some wood, leaving her to drink her tea. I did a quick walk around along the edge of the clearing and collected some sticks. When I got to the section where the tree had been knocked over, I noticed that it had been moved from where it was before. I put my hand on it and crouched down to look at the ground. It was soft and muddy, easy to leave prints and what I saw made my blood run cold, instead of bear paws, like I was expecting, I saw a large human shaped foot, bigger than I had ever seen before. The distinct imprint of toes clearly visible in the deep imprint. I shot up and looked around into the forest but didn't see anything aside from the trees. I quickly walked back to where my girlfriend was putting away her cup and I told her that I felt perhaps it was better to go back today. After everything that happened, I didn't want to risk anything happening to her. She asked me what was wrong and so I brought her over to the imprint, telling her about what my grandfather's friend told me about his seeing sasquatch around here a few years back. She laughed asking if I was playing a joke on her. Her reasoning was that sasquatch was always spotted deep in the States, never in northern Ontario. I shook my head, telling her it wasn't a joke. She looked partially confused at first and then slowly nodded, agreeing with me that we should head back.

My girlfriend quickly got to work on packing up all the food and cooking items we brought. While I worked on emptying the tent before taking it down. As I was finishing up on the tent, we both heard rustling off to our right, in the direction of the fallen tree. We both stopped what we were doing and turned towards the sound. It was hard to see deep into the bush, and I thought it was nothing before spotting movement out of the corner of my eye. I turned to look at it and urged my girlfriend to start loading things into the boat. I could hear her behind me, continuing to keep a close eye on where I saw movement. I didn't see anything else moving and slowly stood up, I grabbed the tent bag and took a step back. I felt a hand on my arm and jumped in fear, whirling around, I saw my girlfriend who said the boat was full and ready. I took her hand and started to walk towards the boat when I was stopped by my girl-friend's face.

It had gone completely pale, looking at something behind me. I slowly turned and what I saw, I will never forget. A man, but much taller than any man I had ever seen, covered in thick fur, its face distorted like a cross between a bear and a monkey with long sharp teeth and deep brown eyes. I sucked in a breath and slowly began backing away, pulling my girlfriend along and trying not to make any sudden movements. I quickly checked behind me and noticed we were close to the boat, turning back towards the creature, it had taken a step forward, now in the clearing with us. Luckily it was still only watching as I began untying the boat, my girlfriend climbing in. I put the tent down gently and gave the boat a soft push, it barely budged. I silently cursed and took a deep breath. I silently counted to three, still watching the creature before turning and pushing as hard as I could. The boat slid free of the ground and into the water, I leapt into the boat as I heard the creature start running towards us. I grabbed the paddle and with a few heavy strokes pushed us a good way away from the shoreline. I turned and looked back, the creature stopping at the edge of the water and screeched at us. It sounded like nails on a chalkboard. I began pulling the cord to start the engine. First try nothing, second try, still nothing. I grabbed the small pump on the gas hose and pumped it a few times. I heard a splash off to our left, the creature tried to throw a stick at us but luckily it landed in the water.

The third try finally brought the engine to life. I quickly turned it to full throttle as my girlfriend and I took off down the lake. We sat in silence until we reached the boat launch. I got out and pulled the boat up, checking on my girlfriend who was shaken up, otherwise fine. We quickly got the truck loaded and drove back to town. On our drive we decided to tell everyone we called the trip early because of a bear, who would believe us if we told them we saw bigfoot. We spent the rest of our vacation at the house, not going out for anything aside from trips to the store and the library to rent a couple movies. We went back home not long after and never again brought it up until now. Ever since then we have never gone back to stinger lake, still taking our yearly trips to Nakina, but always staying at the house.

CHAPTER TEN
IT WAS UGLY

BACK IN APPROXIMATELY 1984, WHEN I WAS JUST A SEVEN-year-old child, I experienced a profoundly intense encounter that remains etched in my memory to this day. It happened quite unexpectedly while I was engrossed in play within the depths of the woods. Little did I know that this innocent adventure would lead me to cross paths with something unimaginable. Startled by my sudden presence, the creature and I found ourselves locked in a chilling stare, mere feet apart, for what felt like an eternity, but was likely only a minute or so. My body was frozen in fear, unable to move or even utter a sound. Then, with a thunderous roar, it broke the spell, jolting me out of my petrified state. Without a second thought, I fled as fast as my legs could carry me, never daring to glance back until I reached the safety of my home, where I struggled to put into words the harrowing encounter that had just unfolded.

What struck me as particularly unique about this encounter was our vantage points. We were situated on a steep incline, with me positioned above and the creature below. As a result, our respective heights were somewhat adjusted, bringing us closer to eye level. Even from my elevated position, looking somewhat downward at the creature, it did nothing to diminish its immense size and intimidating presence.

The memory of that encounter replays in my mind like an unchanging tape, haunting me for over three decades. Even now, every time the recollection resurfaces, it leaves me trembling inside. At that tender age, I had never heard of Bigfoot or any similar creature. What stood before me was simply a monster—a real, terrifying monster. I resided in a small, rural town in Southeastern Wisconsin, a place where the notion of such creatures seemed utterly inconceivable. It was the 80s, a time before the internet and before cable television graced our homes. It wasn't until years later, when cable finally arrived, that I stumbled upon a TV show featuring Bigfoot. As I witnessed the depictions on the screen, I was struck with absolute certainty that what I had encountered all those years ago was exactly the same creature. It defied logic, as my rational mind argued that these beings, if they truly existed, should only reside in vast wilderness areas like the Pacific Northwest or Alaska. I believed that it would be impossible for them to go unnoticed in an area like Wisconsin, devoid of mountains that could provide more inaccessible territories. In an attempt to rationalize my experience, I tried to convince myself that what I saw was a bear. Yet, the face of the creature remained vividly etched in my mind, and deep down, I knew with absolute certainty that there was a 0% chance it was a bear.

One depiction that closely resembles what I saw is a sketch I once came across, which you had posted, featuring two variations of gigantopithecus side by side —one labeled "temperate" and the other labeled "tropical." The temperate depiction bears a striking resemblance to what I encountered. However, I must clarify that many other depictions of gigantopithecus that I have come across do not resemble what I saw. They more closely resemble conventional apes rather than bipedal creatures. The characteristics that resonate with my memory include the hooded nose, the small eyes positioned closely together, the prominent brow ridge, the upright posture, the extensive hair coverage and length, the broad shoulders with a forward-set head giving the appearance of a "no neck," and the long arms reminiscent of primates. Moreover, there is something about the facial expression that evokes a sense of famil-iarity. However, I must admit that what I witnessed was simply far "uglier" than any depiction I have come across.

As the years have passed, I have often pondered the significance of that encounter. It has fueled my curiosity and ignited a desire to explore the uncharted territories that lie beyond the boundaries of our understanding. While I cannot provide concrete proof or claim to have all the answers, I remain steadfast in my conviction that what I encountered was a creature that defies our conventional knowledge—a being that continues to roam the fringes of our known world, leaving us to wonder what other mysteries lie in wait, concealed by our own skepticism.

CHAPTER ELEVEN
I THINK IT WAS A SASQUATCH

I'VE BEEN GRAPPLING WITH A DILEMMA LATELY, UNCERTAIN about whether I should share the incredible experience that has been weighing on my mind. On one hand, there is a strong desire within me to confide in someone, to express the profound encounter that has left me awestruck. On the other hand, the mere thought of describing what I saw makes me question my own sanity, fearing that I might be perceived as a delusional individual. But I can no longer suppress the need to share my story and seek validation.

Over the years, I've immersed myself in a plethora of shows and documentaries, eagerly absorbing every piece of information related to extraordinary phenomena. However, despite my extensive exposure to these accounts, I have yet to come across a description that aligns with what I witnessed.

To put it frankly, what I saw defies categorization. It was an enigmatic figure, a towering presence resembling a very muscular old man with pronounced physical features. Its prominent brow ridge, large mouth, receding hairline, and the entirety of its body covered in a patchwork of brown and gray hair, some parts even translucent. Its most striking characteristic was its incredible height, standing at approximately 7 feet tall. And that's not all. There was something else, a fleeting glimpse of movement behind cover—a sight that revealed golden blonde hair, almost luminous in its radiance.

It's important to emphasize that this entity bore an uncanny resemblance to a man, not an ape or a gorilla. The clarity with which I saw it cannot be denied. From a mere 30 feet away, without any obstructions hindering my view, I observed it in broad daylight. I witnessed the astonishing moment when it rose to its full height, pivoted gracefully, and executed two one-footed jumps that carried it effortlessly into the depths of the surrounding woods, spanning an impressive distance of 20 feet. One of these leaps even involved launching itself onto and off the side of a standing tree, akin to a skilled parkour runner navigating an obstacle or attempting to clear an imaginary gap.

I can already anticipate the skepticism and confusion my account might elicit. Yes, I've heard the term "dirty apes" used before, and I am familiar with the iconic footage from the '60s or '70s that often comes to mind when discussing these elusive creatures. However, what I encountered bears no resemblance to those representations. It defied the conventional imagery associated with Sasquatch or other similar entities. Instead, what stood before me was an extraordinary, mind-boggling sight—an agile and athletic 7-foot-tall naked figure, covered from head to toe in a thick coat of hair, roaming the woods at the early hour of 5:45 in the morning. It sounds utterly unbelievable, I know, but I swear on my own sanity that this is what I witnessed.

And now, I find myself grappling with the question of whether this encounter falls within the realm of a Sasquatch sighting or if it belongs to an entirely different classification of extraordinary beings. The uncertainty gnaws at me, fueling my desire to seek feedback and validation from those who may possess a deeper understanding of these mysteries.

If you have any insights or guidance to offer, I would be immensely grateful. It is essential for me to navigate through this labyrinth of uncertainty, to find solace in knowing that I am not alone in this extraordinary encounter and that there are others who can shed light on the enigma I have experienced.

CHAPTER TWELVE
ENCOUNTER ON THE ROAD

IT WAS SEPTEMBER 30, 2013, AND I FOUND MYSELF DRIVING along Route 109, halfway between Hoquiam and Ocean Shores in Washington. I had just finished my visit to Hoquiam and was heading back to my home in Ocean Shores when an unexpected encounter would forever etch itself into my memory.

As I continued along the road, a deer suddenly darted across, heading south, about an eighth of a mile ahead of me. Being familiar with the behavior of these creatures, I knew that where there was one deer, there was often another close behind. I instinctively slowed down, exercising caution. However, what appeared next left me completely dumbfounded.

Instead of a second deer, an entirely different figure emerged from the edge of the road. This figure, a male being, sprinted across the road with astonishing speed, covering the distance in just three strides. I was taken aback, my mind racing to comprehend what I was witnessing. I brought my vehicle to a complete stop, utterly shocked by the surreal sight before me.

This enigmatic being reached the top of the roadside berm and turned to face me. In that moment, our eyes locked, and a rush of unsettling emotions coursed through me. His grin was unmistakably menacing, leaving me with an undeniable sense of threat. Without further hesitation, he pivoted back around and vanished into the dense brush that lined the roadside.

I had just encountered a Sasquatch, up close and personal. The encounter was so intimate that I could have reached out and touched him, as my car window was rolled down, placing me no more than 20 feet away. His facial features were remarkably human-like, except for the absence of a chin and a pronounced brow ridge. His nose, though human in shape, possessed a slightly European rather than African appearance. Piercing black eyes met my gaze, while his skin and hair exhibited shades of gray. The remnants of teeth he revealed were akin to those of a human, albeit in a severely deteriorated condition. It was clear that oral hygiene was not a priority for him.

Observing his movements provided further insight

into his uniqueness. When he ran, his palms faced downward, unlike our upright thumbs-up position. And when he stood upright, his palms were oriented backward, in contrast to the forward-facing thumbs of a human. Additionally, his arms appeared slightly longer than those of a typical human, though not excessively so—merely half a hand's length beyond what one might expect. As the encounter unfolded during midday, with the sun casting its rays from the south, I could discern the shape of his head through the hair. Although the hair rose significantly, giving the impression of a pointed head, the underlying structure was undeniably human. Roughly estimating his height, I would venture to say he stood between 7 to 8 feet tall. Unfortunately, the encounter transpired too swiftly for me to capture photographic evidence. It was a fleeting moment, but one that would forever remain vivid in my mind.

Furthermore, there were additional peculiarities that caught my attention. As previously mentioned, his hands turned inward more than a human's, and his arms exhibited a slight elongation. The face, nose, and teeth resembled those of a human, while the absence of a chin further distinguished his appearance. These details served to further cement the profound uniqueness of this remarkable being.

Since that fateful day, I have replayed the encounter countless times in my mind, attempting to reconcile the disbelief and awe that gripped me. It was a remarkable experience, one that defied conventional explanations and expanded my understanding of the world around me.

Thank you for allowing me to share.

CHAPTER THIRTEEN
I'M STILL SHOOK UP

LET ME TAKE YOU BACK TO MAY 21, 2011, A DAY THAT WILL forever be etched in my memory. It was on this day that I had a confirmed sighting, an encounter that shook me to my core. But before I delve into the details of that momentous event, I must mention the strange occurrences that have been unfolding in this area since 2010, setting the stage for what was to come.

As I recount this experience, please bear with me as my emotions are still raw and my recollection vivid. Every moment of that encounter remains etched in my mind, as if it happened just yesterday. I remember the uncertainty that filled me, the fear mingled with curiosity, as I grappled with the anticipation of what this mysterious creature would do next. It stood a mere 50 yards away from me, observing my every move. I watched intently as it swiftly maneuvered behind some thick brush near a colossal boulder on the hill, its gaze fixed upon me.

Allow me to paint a picture of what I witnessed. The creature stood tall, measuring between 6 to 7 feet in height. Its head had an ovalish shape, framed by reddish to dark brown fur. I vividly recall the sunlight glinting off its broad shoulders, which were as substantial as those of a linebacker donning full gear. Its eyes, amber-brown in color, stared straight into my soul, unyielding and penetrating. The creature possessed a flat face, and its long, matted hair exuded an air of wildness. It felt as though those immense eyes were peering through me, leaving me paralyzed in fear until the surge of adrenaline finally spurred me into action.

Without a moment's hesitation, I ran. I hurled myself down the hill, approximately 8 feet above the road, desperate to reach the safety of my car. I called out to my friend, who was with me by the river, urging them to join me immediately. "Get into the car now," I pleaded, my voice trembling with urgency. We needed to leave, to escape the presence that had shaken us to our very core. I didn't stop until I reached the sanctuary of my home, far away from the haunting depths of those woods. It was supposed to be a day of leisure, swim-ming, and fishing along the tranquil waters of the

Applegate River. Yet, our time there was cut short, lasting no more than an hour. The proximity of the encounter to my home, a mere 60 miles away, rendered the trip seemingly wasteful in terms of time and gas. The adrenaline coursing through my veins propelled me to speed back home, my foot heavy on the accelerator.

You may wonder why I am so certain that this encounter was no ordinary encounter with a bear or a cougar. Allow me to clarify. A bear would have swiftly vanished into the depths of the woods before I even registered its presence, as they possess a keen awareness of their surroundings. Similarly, a mountain lion would have likely chosen a different fate for me, making it impossible for me to share this account. No, what I witnessed that day was something entirely different. It was a creature that defied the natural order, for it stood upright on two legs. Growing up amidst the wilderness and forests of the Pacific Northwest, I have encountered countless creatures that inhabit our planet. Yet, this being was like nothing I had ever seen before, except in the grainy videos capturing elusive sightings. It resembled Patty, the infamous figure captured on film, forever etched in the annals of Bigfoot lore. The encounter left me unsettled, unsure if it meant harm. But to me, in that moment, it exuded an undeniable sense of threat.

It is important to note that there have been many

unspoken sightings in the Red Buttes Wilderness, an expansive region stretching from the Oregon/California border to Highway 96 in Siskyou County. This area encompasses Saied Valley, Happy Camp, Indian Creek Road, Oregon Caves National Monument, and countless other locations. I stumbled upon a report shared by a hippy farmer from Talkemla, who revealed a deeply ingrained understanding of the Bigfoot phenomenon. He and his companions, from their earliest days, had been warned about the presence of these enigmatic creatures in the area. According to him, they are highly territorial and known to be aggressive. Venturing into this domain means subjecting oneself to the possibility, or rather the danger, of encountering one of these elusive beings.

So, as I share my story with you, I do so not just to recount my personal encounter, but also to shed light on the broader tapestry of sightings and unspoken experiences that have woven themselves into the fabric of this region. We find ourselves at the threshold of an ancient mystery, one that demands our attention and exploration. It is my hope that by sharing my account, I can contribute to the collective knowledge surrounding these elusive creatures and perhaps unravel a fragment of the enigma that has haunted these lands for generations.

CHAPTER FOURTEEN
IT ATTACKED OUR CAMP

FOUR YEARS AGO, IN LATE AUGUST 2019, MY FAMILY AND I made the decision to go camping on our property which happens to border federal and BLM land.

Our property is beautiful but the BLM land has a splendor we all love. It's a nature reserve, teeming with wildlife. It's not uncommon to encounter deer, turkey, foxes, and a variety of other indigenous animals, who have grown so accustomed to human presence that they willingly approach for hand-feeding. The area boasts a strict no-hunting policy, allowing these creatures to flourish undisturbed. Among its notable features are the labyrinthine caves and babbling creeks that crisscross the landscape. In fact, the creek bordering our property holds historical significance, having been named by none other than Squire Boone and frequented by the

Boone family. Furthermore, abandoned mills, remnants of a bygone era, silently narrate their stories, with some even having been constructed by Abraham Lincoln's father. It is within this rich tapestry of natural wonders and American history that our camping adventure unfolded.

As we set up camp that evening, an unusual occurrence caught our attention. We noticed rocks rolling on the ground at various points during the night. Initially, I worried that someone might be lurking in the woods, deliberately throwing stones. However, given the remote and rural nature of our community, such an event would have been highly unlikely.

Adding to our perplexity was the presence of a haunting sound, reverberating through the night. It resembled a mix between a woman's scream and a wolf's howl, far deeper and louder than the familiar yelps of foxes we were accustomed to hearing.

As the hour grew late, my children grew weary and decided to retire to their tent. My eldest son insisted on using his own dome camping tent, a decision that made me feel uneasy, despite our seemingly safe surroundings. To alleviate my concerns, I requested that he position his tent within direct view of our family tent's window, allowing me to keep a watchful eye on him.

Exhausted, I entered my own tent after extinguishing the fire, seeking solace in its warmth while awaiting the arrival of dawn. The time was approximately 2 a.m.

Suddenly, a peculiar sound emanated from outside the tent, originating from the depths of the surrounding woods. I discerned a cracking noise accompanied by heavy footsteps trampling through the grass. The sequence went, "WHOOOSH thump WHOOOSH thump WHOOOOSH THUMP," prompting a chuckle to escape my lips. I assumed it was a deer or raccoons, their arrival coinciding with our retreat to slumber. However, my amusement was short-lived, for the sound was distinctly bipedal. Moreover, an unpleasant odor wafted into the air—an amalgamation of wet dog and skunk, reminiscent of the pungency one encounters in an elephant pen at the zoo. Suddenly, my tent began to jolt as if being repeatedly bumped from the outside. The creature continued its relentless advance, heading directly toward my son's tent. Without warning, the unimaginable occurred—my son's entire tent lifted off the ground, suspended in the air as if weightless. It shook violently, while my son screamed in terror, desperately pleading for it to stop. It's important to note that my other son, who was 14 at the time, had fallen ill and retired early due to him not feeling well. It was inconceivable that this massive entity could be my son, considering the tent was elevated several feet above the ground.

Fearful for my son's life I shouted loudly for it to go away.

In response to my outcry, the creature abruptly released the tent, causing it to crash back to the ground. It swiftly retraced its steps, running with astonishing speed toward my tent, which once again became the target of its forceful bumps. Then, with a resounding "WHOOSH thump" and the unmistakable sound of branches breaking, it vanished into the depths of the woods.

My son immediately sought refuge in my tent, and together, we phoned my husband, who was returning home from his night shift job.

Fast forward to the next year, mid-October 2020. My son and daughter were outside our home when an overpowering stench enveloped them. Even with both garage doors wide open, the putrid odor permeated the air. Curiosity piqued, my son ventured out to investigate the source of the foul smell. To our astonishment, an enormous creature, draped in dark fur with its eyes illuminated by the porch lights, stood in the middle of our yard—merely ten feet away from the very spot where the tent incident had unfolded four years prior.

In a moment of realization, my other son

approached me and declared that the description of this creature matched precisely what he and his friend had encountered near our creek. It had been hunched over at the water's edge, but as they drew closer, it swiftly rose onto two legs and briskly retreated into the depths of the woods.

As someone who typically requires concrete evidence before embracing extraordinary claims, I must confess that I have now become a believer. This journey has transformed me, unveiling a realm of mystery and wonder that lies just beyond the veil of our everyday existence.

CHAPTER FIFTEEN
READY TO TELL MY STORY

WHAT I'M ABOUT TO DETAIL TOOK PLACE IN THE EARLY 1970s. I have refrained from sharing it often and have told others who write or talk about this sort of thing. I wanted to share with you in the event you want to put it in your book.

————

We had parked the truck and decided to take a break from our hunting expedition. Placing our lunch on the hood of the vehicle, we stood around, occasionally pacing, as we enjoyed our meal. The road leading to the ramp was newly constructed, about 25 feet wide, and flanked by cleared timber spanning approximately 30 to

40 feet on each side. From the ramp, the road stretched straight ahead for a good 400 yards.

The day was perfect for hunting, with the sun shining brightly and clear skies above. The air was filled with the melodious songs of birds, adding to the serenity of the moment. As we savored our meal and basked in the beauty of our surroundings, an unpleasant odor suddenly assailed our senses. It was a putrid stench akin to that of an outhouse. We scanned the area, trying to locate the source, but nothing unusual came into view.

However, the stench grew increasingly intense, prompting us to gaze down the road. To our astonishment, we spotted a dark figure, human-like in shape but far too large to be a man, traversing the clearing about 200 to 250 yards away from us. The creature emerged from the woods along the river, moving deliberately with long strides. What struck us most was the way it held its forearms parallel to the ground, as if carrying something, although we couldn't discern any object in its grasp. The witness suggested that due to the creature's midsection being covered in long hair, it might have concealed a small animal, held close to its body and blending with its fur color.

Remarkably, the creature never acknowledged our presence and swiftly crossed the cleared area and roadbed. It took mere seconds for it to traverse the entire opening. Its stride left a lasting impression on us, as each step covered an impressive distance of over eight feet, all without any signs of running. In just around 12 steps, the creature disappeared into the depths of the woods.

Feeling a sense of unease, my father retrieved his shotgun from the truck's cab, loaded it, and placed it on the hood. He kept a watchful eye on the woods while we finished our lunch, but we didn't catch sight of the creature again. Later that afternoon, we returned the boat to the river and continued hunting until darkness fell, encountering no further incidents.

As for the creature's description, it stood at a towering height of over eight feet, possibly even reaching nine. Its body was covered in shaggy and patchy hair, predominantly rusty-red with black streaks dispersed throughout. The hair wasn't sleek but rather had a rough texture. Notably, the hair on its legs, back, sides, and midsection appeared longer than that on its upper shoulders and head. Unfortunately, we never got a full view of its face. The creature's head seemed to rest directly on its shoulders, lacking a distinct neck, resulting in a shape reminiscent of a "dinner bell," with the shoulder muscles sloping up to form the flared lower part of the "bell." In a way, the positioning of the head on the shoulders resembled that of a large gorilla.

Its chest and shoulders were massive, exuding strength and power. We noticed that the upper arms, from shoulder to elbow, seemed noticeably shorter than the lower arms extending from the elbow to the hand. The waist, while not exceptionally narrow, appeared more shaggy and adorned with longer hair. There was no discernible evidence to determine the creature's gender, but both of us believed it to be male.

CHAPTER SIXTEEN
FACE TO FACE WITH A SASQUATCH

In September of 2012, I decided to take a three-day vacation from Northern Nevada to the Southern Coast of Oregon. As a photographer for my website, I wanted to capture some stunning scenic shots before the weather turned cold and dreary for the rest of the year.

Accompanied by my fiance, we embarked on a hike about six to eight miles above Brookings, Oregon, in Curry County. Our chosen path led us through a densely wooded area, following the loop trail located approximately a quarter mile past the renowned Natural Bridges viewpoint.

Initially, our hike proceeded without any notable incidents, although the diminishing daylight prompted a sense of urgency to hasten our return, despite no logical reason to do so. It was an inexplicable feeling, as if the hairs on the back of my neck stood on end. I struggled to articulate the discomfort that washed over me. Along the trail, we didn't encounter any fellow hikers during our ascent or descent.

It was when we paused after hearing loud snaps echoing through the forest, resembling the sound of branches breaking, that our unease heightened. Initially, we couldn't spot anything amiss. Resolving to continue walking, we suddenly noticed bushes about twenty yards ahead swaying back and forth. Sensing something was off, we stopped once more, only to be assaulted by a repugnant stench reminiscent of rotting garbage festering under the scorching sun.

By then, my initial nervousness had escalated, compounded by the encroaching fog and fading light. The misty forest became veiled in a light rain. Struggling up a steep section of the trail, I exerted all my effort to reach its end.

As we neared the final ascent, a compulsion led me to glance behind me, despite not fully understanding why. It felt as if I were being watched, although I chastised myself for entertaining such notions. To my astonishment, I glimpsed a head rising above the tree branches, its body concealed by the dense vegetation. The head was adorned with dark reddish-brown fur and positioned at an impossible height above the ground. If this figure was a man, he must have stood close to eight feet tall. I blinked repeatedly, questioning my own sanity, hoping it was a mere figment of my imagination.

Yet, the creature I beheld didn't vanish into thin air. Instead, it regarded me with a curious gaze for a few fleeting seconds before disappearing from sight behind a tree. Gripping my fiance's hand tightly, too frightened to disclose what I had witnessed, fearing he might venture in search of it, I hurried back to our vehicle as swiftly as possible. I assure you, I am not delusional. This was no optical illusion caused by light or fog. Something immense, with an ape-like face, observed me intently.

The memory of that encounter remains etched in my mind forever. Strangely, the forest fell eerily silent a few minutes prior to the incident. The crickets ceased their chirping, the birds muted their melodies, and a profound stillness enveloped everything. We attributed it to the onset of the light rainfall, but it felt as if nature itself held its breath in that moment.

CHAPTER SEVENTEEN
ENCOUNTER IN THE SIERRA NEVADA MOUNTAINS

THIS IS A TRUE STORY FROM MY PAST, AN EXPERIENCE THAT HAS stayed with me for over 20 years. As someone who loves backpacking and has explored remote areas in the western states, encountering various wildlife, including grizzly bears, I had never encountered anything as strange as what happened on this particular occasion.

It was late summer 1989, a Friday evening after work. I decided to venture out alone, accompanied by my dogs. My destination was White Rock Lake in Tahoe National Forest, a place I had never been to before. The challenge was finding the lake since the roads were unmarked. According to the topo map, I could reach it via a 4-wheel drive road.

I found myself driving slowly on rough, rocky dirt roads, trying to figure out my location. The roads seemed to fade away or intersect with other 4-wheel drive paths, leaving me disoriented. I was in the middle of nowhere, with no lakes, significant creeks, or clear destinations in sight for miles.

Deciding to wait until daylight to avoid further confusion in the darkness, I pulled my 4-wheel drive pickup off the road, although I probably didn't need to since I hadn't seen anyone or anything. I parked a few yards away from the rocky road, hidden by the surrounding trees. I grabbed my sleeping bag and laid it out in front of my truck, settling down with my dogs under the starry night sky.

Sometime in the early morning, around 3 or 4 a.m., while it was still pitch black, I woke up to the sound of something walking towards me on the road. It was a heavy, steady footfall, clearly bipedal in nature. At first, I assumed it might be another backpacker, given the rhythm of the steps. But then I questioned why someone would be out here on this road in the middle of the night, without light, surrounded by miles of dense forest. Although I knew it wasn't a bear (I had encountered many bears in the wild), I couldn't identify what it could be. Nonetheless, I still thought a backpacker was the most reasonable explanation.

As the sound grew closer, I pondered whether I should say something, but I didn't want to startle anyone unnecessarily. I convinced myself that the passerby would simply continue on without noticing me. However, my growing nervousness was unusual, as there aren't many things in the wilderness that make me feel that way. Strangely, my dogs remained silent and motionless, which added to the suspense. Typically, they would have at least barked as a warning. This heavy bipedal entity continued approaching, getting closer to the spot where I had parked my truck off the road. I lay there, holding my breath. I didn't know what to expect and hoped it would pass by without even realizing I was there. The darkness obscured my vision completely.

As it drew nearer, I could sense its size, as the rhythm of its footsteps indicated a significant presence. In my nervousness, I remained utterly silent. At that moment, a thought of encountering a sasquatch didn't cross my mind. I had never given much thought to such things, especially in the Sierras. But that was about to change. The entity reached the point where my truck was parked off the road... and suddenly, silence. It stopped. Although I couldn't see it in the darkness, it stood only a few yards away from where I lay in my sleeping bag.

I'm not sure if I made a sound or if one of my dogs did, but something triggered a reaction from it. The entity emitted the most horrifying, piercing scream imaginable—a scream that defies description. It had lungs like nothing I had ever encountered before. Then, still screaming, it turned around and ran back down the road in the darkness at an astonishing speed. It continued to scream, the sound echoing through the forest without ceasing. I could hear the screams fading in the distance.

I lay there in complete shock, unable to believe what had just transpired. Eventually, I snapped out of it and quickly gathered my belongings, tossing them into my truck. My dogs were equally disturbed by the experience. I assumed the entity had moved far away by then, so before leaving the area, I drove down the road with my brights on, attempting to find any footprints or signs of something unusual. My adrenaline was pumping. Although I didn't actually step out of the truck, I opened the door and peered down, hoping to spot footprints or any clue about what I had encountered. The road was too rocky to show any prints. I then let my dogs out, hoping they might pick up a scent (although I didn't know what I would do if they did), but strangely, they immediately jumped back into the truck. This was out of character for them. I tried once more, but they insisted on staying inside. Realizing they were as unnerved as I was, I knew it was time to get out of there.

I drove several miles back toward the main road, my adrenaline still surging.

Before this experience, I hadn't given much thought to sasquatches, but now I'm definitely a believer. People try to explain it away, but I know what I heard. I didn't see anything, nor did I detect any unusual odor, but it was so close that I could feel its presence. And when it screamed, it was so close that I'm surprised I didn't feel the spit from its mouth. Nothing in those forests could scream like that or run that fast, especially nothing walking upright. I don't dwell on the subject of sasquatch, nor have I made it my mission to search for them, but I know they exist. My experience is still vivid in my mind. Whether or not others believe it is irrelevant to me. I'm not sharing this account to convince anyone; I'm simply sharing an experience I had one night in the Sierras near Truckee.

CHAPTER EIGHTEEN
MEN STEALERS

INTERESTING HISTORICAL ACCOUNT SENT IN FROM A READER.

———

Elkanah Walker, born on August 7, 1805, was an American pioneer settler who played a significant role in the early development of the Oregon Country, encompassing present-day Oregon and Washington states. He grew up on a farm near North Yarmouth, Maine, being the sixth child of Jeremiah and Jane Walker. Elkanah's thirst for knowledge led him to attend the Bangor Theological Seminary.

Elkanah and his family embarked on a journey to the Oregon Country, joining a group of missionaries who were also seeking to spread their teachings in the region. From August 1838 to June 1848, Elkanah Walker, along with his colleague Cushing Eells and their wives, established and resided at the Tshimakain Mission. This mission, supported by the American Board of Commissioners for Foreign Missions, aimed to study the local language and introduce the Protestant faith to the Spokane People, a Native American tribe residing in the area.

During their time at the Tshimakain Mission, Elkanah Walker and his companions immersed themselves in the local culture and language, working diligently to build relationships with the Spokane People. Their mission involved not only religious teachings but also education and community development. They sought to improve the lives of the Spokane People through their efforts, providing education and healthcare services alongside spreading their Protestant beliefs.

Through their dedication and perseverance, Elkanah Walker and Cushing Eells left a lasting impact on the Spokane People and the wider Oregon Country. They played a crucial role in bridging cultural gaps, promoting understanding, and contributing to the social and spiritual growth of the region. Elkanah Walker's legacy as a pioneer settler and missionary is remembered as a significant chapter in the early history of the Oregon Country.

In his diary he had an interesting section something they natives feared called, The Men Stealers.

Elkanah wrote in diary the following:

"Bear with me if I trouble you with a little of their superstitions. They believe in a race of giants, which inhabit a certain mountain off to the west of us. This mountain is covered with perpetual snow. They (the creatures) inhabit the snow peaks. They hunt and do all their work at night. They are men stealers.

They come to the people's lodges at night when the people are asleep and take them and put them under their skins and to their place of abode without even waking. Their track is a foot and a half long. They steal salmon from Indian nets and eat them raw as the bears do. If the people are awake, they always know when they are coming very near by their strong smell that is most intolerable. It is not uncommon for them to come in the night and give three whistles and then the stones will begin to hit their houses."

Reverend Walker's mission was situated around twenty-five miles northwest of what is now Spokane, Washington. In his diary entry, he described a snow-capped peak to the west, which could have referred to several mountains in the Cascade Range. It is possible that he was observing mountains like Mt. Baker, Mt. Rainier, Mt. Adams, or even Mount St. Helens. Alternatively, he might have been referring to Mt. Hood, located on the Oregon side of the Columbia River. The exact mountain he was describing remains uncertain, as the region was surrounded by majestic peaks, each with its own distinct beauty.

CHAPTER NINETEEN
BIGFOOT EATING

Bigfoot was never something I gave much thought to, especially growing up in Louisiana. Sure, I had heard stories about it as a kid, but I always considered them to be nothing more than tales. Little did I know that my perspective was about to change on that fateful spring day.

Craving some peace and quiet away from the hustle and bustle of daily life, I decided to go for a solitary walk. Nature has always been my solace, a place where I could find serenity. I made my way down to the Red River, a spot I often frequented during my strolls. As I walked, I consciously tuned my senses, focusing on the sounds and sights around me. I took pleasure in the simple act of listening.

When I arrived at the edge of the bridge overlooking

the river, something caught my eye. There, squatting by the water's edge, was a figure. Initially, my thoughts raced to the possibility of encountering a homeless person or a local enjoying the outdoors. However, as I observed more closely, I noticed that this individual was covered in hair from head to toe. Confusion washed over me. Why would someone be donning a Bigfoot costume in such a secluded area? My eyes darted around, half-expecting to see hidden cameras or mischievous teenagers orchestrating a prank. But there was no one else in sight, no evidence of a hoax.

My attention turned back to the mysterious figure, and as I continued to watch, details began to emerge. It was engrossed in breaking open mussels or clams, whatever it could find in the river. I couldn't help but wonder why someone would eat them raw from such a polluted and trash-laden waterway. That's when it hit me like a thunderbolt: this was no ordinary human. The realization sunk in, and a shiver ran down my spine.

The creature continued its primitive feast, completely oblivious to my presence. It never once turned to face me, and I stood frozen, transfixed by the encounter. In that moment, I made a decision to quietly retreat and rush back home to retrieve my phone. I desperately wanted to capture this astonishing sight on camera, but by the time I returned to the bridge, darkness had enveloped the surroundings, and the creature was gone without a trace.

What struck me most about the creature was its appearance. Covered in a dense coat of brown hair or fur, it remained squatting the entire time, displaying an impressive feat of balance and stability. I, on the other hand, struggled to hold a squat position for more than a few seconds. Its hands, though resembling human hands in shape, possessed a darker color and a texture reminiscent of gorillas or apes. The creature's height was difficult to ascertain accurately, but it appeared to be on the younger side, perhaps standing around 6 or 7 feet tall. To determine its true size, I would need someone to assist me in measuring.

As I made my way back home that evening, a whirl-wind of thoughts and emotions consumed me. The encounter had shattered my skepticism and thrust me into a world of unknown possibilities. Bigfoot, a creature once dismissed as mere folklore, had become an enigma that demanded further exploration and under-standing.

CHAPTER TWENTY
IT ATTACKED OUR CAMPER

In 2011, my family and I went on a hunt near the Grand Canyon. We set up camp close to where our family had a strange encounter before.

On Friday night, around 9 pm, my sister and I walked down the road from camp and made some noises, like howling and whooping, hoping to get a response. We tried for about 30 minutes but didn't hear anything back, so we returned to camp.

When we got back, my sister took my daughter and nephew into the camp trailer to put them to bed. Just as they went inside, things started to get exciting. My brother and I were sitting by the campfire, talking, when we heard a loud crash, like a large branch breaking off a tree, or something stepping on a big branch. It was so loud that we both noticed it. We tried to act casual and just listened for any more sounds while continuing our conversation.

For the next 30 minutes or so, we heard something circling our camp. There were two separate things, and they weren't being quiet. They were making a lot of noise, breaking branches and rustling in the trees. One of them paced back and forth behind the camp trailer, while the other moved from the northwest side of the camp towards the east. Sometimes we heard what sounded like a smaller tree being shaken, or heavy foot-steps in the tall grass. We could tell there were two of them because we could hear both at the same time doing different things.

Then they started throwing rocks and sticks. The first thing we heard was a stick hitting a tarp we had set up for shade near the trailer. After that, there was a continuous barrage of small rocks and sticks being thrown around the campsite. The biggest rock that was thrown landed between us and the camp trailer with a thud that scared us both. At that point, we decided to go into the trailer for more cover. Inside, my sister and nephew were still awake, and they said they could hear everything we had heard from inside. My sister mentioned hearing footsteps behind the trailer the whole time, and she even heard a loud, heavy sigh at one point. She also heard branches breaking and either rocks or twigs being thrown at the trailer. My nephew confirmed her account, and we all tried to go to sleep.

As we lay in the darkness, we heard a loud metallic thud outside the trailer. There was a metal box with food on a small table, and it sounded like something had either knocked on the box or thrown something hard at it. We eventually fell asleep, except for my brother, who couldn't sleep. He continued to hear things being thrown at the trailer for a while. He did eventually fall asleep but was woken up in the early morning by the sound of something being dragged across the canvas roof of the trailer above his head.

The next day was uneventful as we didn't try making any more calls. My nephew had gotten sick from being so nervous the night before. It rained that night, and another hunting group had set up camp nearby.

On Sunday night, my sister and I went down the road again to make some calls, this time on the opposite side. We repeated our attempts from Friday, but once again, there was no response. We went back to camp and sat around the fire for about 30 minutes without anything happening, and then we went to bed.

During the night, something shook the camper trailer violently at least six times. It felt like someone was grabbing the sides and twisting it forcefully from side to side. It wasn't the wind because the trailer didn't sway in one direction; it was more like someone was deliberately shaking it. All three of us adults felt it throughout the night. My brother also heard a low growl around midnight that lasted about 10 seconds. He described it as a subtle but strong sound, and he could feel the vibrations it produced. It felt like it was slightly shaking him. The next morning, we packed up and headed home.

During the weekend, we checked the camp for any signs or footprints. The ground was covered with thick layers of oak leaves and pine needles. The only things we found were the small sticks and rocks, about 3-4 inches in size, that were used to pelt our trailer.

CHAPTER TWENTY-ONE
IT STARED ME DOWN

My encounter took place in 2021. I've hesitated to share my story for almost two years because the other person who witnessed it doesn't want to be involved or have her name associated with it.

Around 11 am, my friend and I left to go geocaching. (Geocaching is a hobby where you find hidden objects based on GPS coordinates.) We went to a rather popular trail because this is where people will leave caches to find.

The trail in question wass an abandoned railway with overgrown sections, muddy spots, and various surroundings like fields, ponds, streams, trees, roads, homes, and forests.

While on the trail, we passed a church and a graveyard. Inside the graveyard, we found a geocache hidden in a bush. Afterward, we walked across a field of tall grass to return to the trail. We noticed a path of matted down grass, possibly made by deer or other geocachers heading back to the trail from the graveyard.

On the other side of the grassy area, there was a line of trees with a stream beyond it, and then more trees with the rail trail just beyond that. We realized we had to jump across the stream, but it seemed too wide for us. However, we noticed footprints in the mud, indicating someone had made the jump before us. We assumed it was another geocacher.

We followed the stream for a few minutes until we found a narrower spot where we could jump across. Continuing along the rail trail, we found a few more geocaches. Suddenly, a group of turkeys ran out from the bushes on the right side and disappeared into the left side.

I quickly took some photos of the turkeys with my iPhone and asked my friend if she saw them too. As I looked up the trail, I saw a tall figure step out from where the turkeys had emerged. It walked the same path as the turkeys and then stopped, turning its torso to face me directly.

At that moment, I realized it wasn't a person. It

stood about 7-8 feet tall, covered in uneven salt and pepper hair that appeared dark grey and black. Its face was flat, resembling a monkey's face with dark, hairless skin around the eyes, mouth, and nose. I couldn't recall specific facial features as my attention shifted to its left arm, which was bulky and covered in hair. It held a motionless turkey under its arm, as if carrying a football. Before I could make eye contact again, it swiftly moved into the trees.

Later, my friend mentioned that the creature made eye contact with her, wrinkled its nose, and showed its teeth. She didn't provide many additional details about its appearance, and she seemed reluctant to discuss it further. The encounter was completely silent, with no grunts or heavy breathing.

After it disappeared, I realized I could have taken a clear photo since I was around 50-75 feet away from it. However, I was too shocked to remember that my phone was set to the camera app. The distance estimation was based on the geocache app, which showed the location of the next cache near where the creature and turkeys had appeared. The app's accuracy could vary due to poor cellular connection at the time.

Without discussing it, we decided to end our day and returned to our car. I've tried talking to my friend about the sighting, but she refuses to discuss it. She made it clear that if I choose to share my story, I should use pseudonyms and exclude her from any mention because she doesn't want anyone knowing what she did or didn't see.

Thank you for allowing me to share.

CHAPTER TWENTY-TWO
THE WOODS MONSTER

BACK IN 1973, WHEN I WAS JUST 11 YEARS OLD, MY FAMILY AND I lived east of Knoxville, Tennessee. It was a pretty sparsely populated area, and not much exciting stuff happened there. However, one day my younger brother and his friends came rushing to us, claiming they had seen a bear peeking into the Brad's house. Well, you can imagine how intrigued us older kids were by that news. We immediately hopped on our bikes and pedaled down the old highway towards the Brad's house, hoping to catch a glimpse of the bear ourselves.

As we were cycling along the road, something big and dark suddenly crossed our path and disappeared into the woods. One of my friends shouted that it wasn't a bear, but actually a man. I wasn't quite sure what it was, but yeah, it was definitely walking on two legs and had a uniform color. We reached the point where we believed it had entered the woods. This was our special trail that led to our fallen tree fort, which we proudly called "The "Hideout". The trail twisted and turned, taking us down into what I guess you could call a canyon or drainage area.

There were lots of trees and vegetation, and there were no houses or people around for quite a distance. I dropped my bike and led the way down the trail, eager to find out where the man was headed and whether he would disturb our fort. We ran down the trail, and as we approached the final bend, I abruptly stopped and glanced down to see something monstrous instead of a man. It had come to a halt near a log bridge that spanned a small dry creek bed. Right at that spot, the trails split, with one going up the draw and the other crossing the log bridge to continue on the opposite side. Our fort was located a bit farther down the trail. So, upon seeing this thing, my first thought was, "This isn't real." I couldn't quite make out what it was until it turned its body and looked up at me. By this time, the other kids had caught up and were piling up behind me, as I had stopped abruptly.

The creature stared at me with a completely expressionless face—no emotions whatsoever. It was bizarre. I turned around and urgently yelled at everyone to scramble back up the trail as fast as they could. We all bolted out of the trailhead, but I struggled to grab my bike and mount it in the rush. Eventually, I gave up and tossed it aside, sprinting all the way back home. The rest of the kids managed to reach our house, some running, some still on their bikes. My friend Sam, who had also seen the creature, asked me what it was. The other kids hadn't seen it, but they were just as frightened as Sam and me. Sam and I told them it was a woods monster, but when I tried to tell my mom the same thing, she dismissed our story.

The things that stuck in my memory were the creature's lack of emotion, which struck me as strange. Any animal or person would surely react in some way to a bunch of kids charging toward them in the woods, right? It had a pointed head with a patch of blonde hair on the left side, but apart from that, I can't recall many other details. I have no idea how big it actually was, what color its skin was, or even the color of its eyes, which I assume were black since I don't remember seeing any white in them. I estimate that it was about forty to fifty yards away from me, down the trail.

When my dad came home, I tried telling him the

whole story, but it didn't really stick with him either. I had to convince him to walk down the road with me to retrieve my bike. After that incident, we never ventured back into the woods. However, a few weeks later, something else happened. We had all bought new pocket knives and were sitting on a ledge, overlooking the canyon/drainage area, whittling sticks and still talking about whether the woods monster was still lurking around. Unfortunately, my pocket knife slipped out of my hand and flew over the ledge, landing amidst the trees and bushes below. We peered over the edge and spotted my new knife lying on the ground. Three of us mustered the courage to make our way down and retrieve it while the others stood watch. Once again, we had to navigate a series of switchbacks to reach the bottom. As we were heading back up the trail, we suddenly heard rustling noises from above, right where we needed to go. Instantly, we all panicked and began running down the main trail that led to the beach. We had never gone all the way to the beach before. After a long sprint, we emerged onto the shoreline and started heading south toward the houses that I knew were there. Finally, we reached the first house, frantically knocked on the door, and a lady answered. We asked to use her phone, and I called my mom to come pick us up.

That encounter with the woods monster and the

subsequent knife incident were unforgettable for all of us. Even though our accounts were dismissed by our parents, we couldn't shake the fear and curiosity that lingered in our minds.

———

CONTINUE WITH

ENCOUNTERS BIGFOOT, VOLUME 2

ABOUT THE AUTHOR

Ethan Hayes grew up in Oklahoma and moved to Texas when he attended Texas A&M. Upon graduation he was hired by Texas Parks and Wildlife and remained there until he retired twenty-two years later. He currently lives in southeast Texas with his wife and two dogs. When he's not spending time enjoying the outdoors and writing, he sips a cold beer on his front porch while listening to Bluegrass music.

———

Send in your encounter story:
encountersbigfoot@gmail.com

ALSO BY ETHAN HAYES

GET THESE SERIES FROM BESTSELLING AUTHOR ETHAN HAYES

ENCOUNTERS IN THE WOODS

WHAT LURKS BEYOND

FEAR IN THE FOREST

INTO THE DARKNESS

ENCOUNTERS BIGFOOT

ALSO BY FREE REIGN PUBLISHING

www.ingramcontent.com/pod-product-compliance
Lightning Source LLC
Chambersburg PA
CBHW052003170626
46808CB00007B/2758